ARTHUR
AND THE
SCHOOL PET

调皮的小沙鼠

（美）马克·布朗　绘著

范晓星　译

CHISO 新疆青少年出版社

It was D.W.'s last day of school
before Christmas vacation.
"Who will take our gerbil
home for the holidays?"
Ms. Morgan asked.

3

"Not us!" said Tommy
and Timmy Tibble.
"Our grandmother said,
'Never again.'"
"I'll take him," said D.W.

"Great," said Ms. Morgan,

"but remember, Speedy is speedy."

"Oh, I'll be very careful," said D.W.

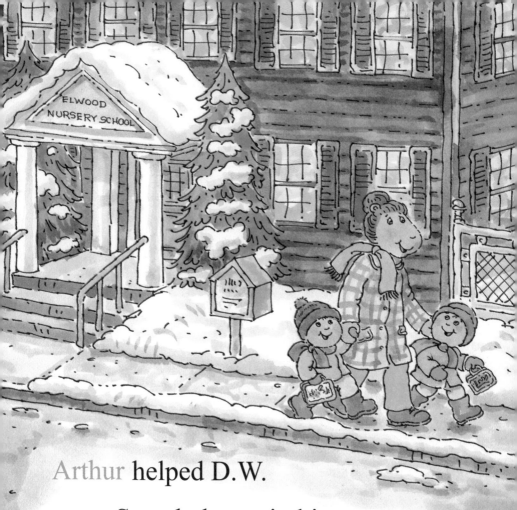

Arthur helped D.W.

carry Speedy home in his cage.

"He's cute," said Arthur.

"He's smart, too," said D.W.

"I'm going to teach him tricks."

"He's not a dog," said Arthur.

"You can't teach gerbils tricks."

D.W. kept Speedy in her room.
"You can't play with him, Arthur,"
she said. "He might get away."

But she played with him.

She tried to teach him

to stand on one paw.

"Be a ballerina," she told him,

"and I'll give you this cheese."

But Speedy just wanted

to eat the cheese.

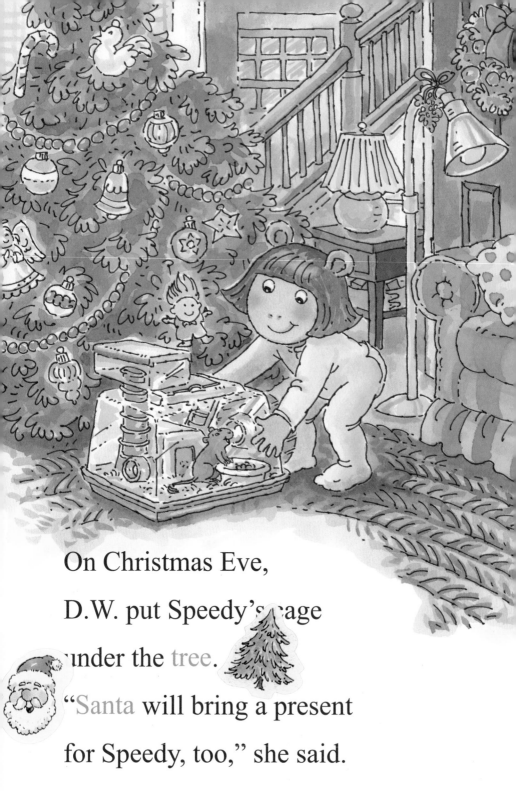

On Christmas Eve,

D.W. put Speedy's cage

under the tree.

"Santa will bring a present

for Speedy, too," she said.

After D.W. went to bed,
Arthur put a piece of cheese
in Speedy's cage.
"Just in case Santa forgets,"
he said to himself.

The next morning, D.W. ran
to see what Santa had left her.
But the first thing she saw
was Speedy's cage.
It was empty!
"HELP!" she screamed.
"Speedy is gone!"

Everyone came running.

They looked under the sofa

and behind the presents

and all around the living room.

D.W. cried harder and harder.

Then Arthur looked up at the tree.

"Look!" shouted Arthur.

"Speedy's on top of the tree!"

He was eating a piece of cheese

and standing on one paw.

"Does he think he's a ballerina?"

laughed Arthur.

"Yes, Smarty-Pants," said D.W.

"I taught him that trick."

Somehow Speedy got out
of his cage three more times.
Once they found him
under the cake box.
He was eating carrot cake.

Once they found him

sleeping in D.W.'s dollhouse.

And once they found him

in Arthur's snow boot.

"I am so glad that school
starts tomorrow," said Mom.
"I need a vacation
from that gerbil."
"I want Speedy
to look very nice
when he goes back to school,"
said D.W.

"So I'm going to give him a bubble bath."

When D.W. said "bath,"

Speedy took off

like lightning!

D.W. and Mom looked everywhere.

So did Arthur and Dad.

They looked upstairs.

They looked downstairs.

They looked in boxes

and drawers and closets.

But no one could find Speedy.

"I can never go to school again!"

cried D.W.

"Don't worry," said Arthur.

"He'll turn up."

But Arthur looked worried.

D.W. got ready for bed.

"Everyone is going to hate me

for losing Speedy," she said.

Then she crawled under the covers.

She felt something warm and furry.

"Speedy!" she whispered.

And there he was—

hiding in her bed!

D.W. arrived at school
with Speedy in his cage.
"Was he much trouble?"
asked Ms. Morgan.
"No problem," said D.W.

译文

2. 圣诞假期的前一天，朵拉班上的摩根老师问大家："谁愿意把我们的小沙鼠快快带回家过圣诞节呀？"

4. "我们可不行！"丁丁和当当异口同声地说，"奶奶说了：'再也不准把小沙鼠带回家！'"

"我带它回家吧。"朵拉说。

5. "很好，"摩根老师点点头，"不过你要记住，快快跑得可不是一般快哦！"

"嗯，我会特别当心的。"朵拉回答。

7. 亚瑟帮朵拉把快快和小鼠笼带回家。

"它真可爱!"亚瑟说。

"它还特别聪明,"朵拉点点头,"我要教它几样本领!"

"它又不是小狗,"亚瑟回应,"小沙鼠什么都学不会的。"

8. 朵拉把快快放在自己的房间里,对亚瑟说:

"你不可以和它玩儿,哥哥,它会溜出来的。"

9. 可是,朵拉自己却和快快玩儿起来。

她想教会它用单脚站立。

"来做芭蕾小明星吧,我给你吃奶酪。"她对快快说。

可惜快快只想吃奶酪。

10. 圣诞前夜，朵拉把快快的小鼠笼放在圣诞树下，说：

"圣诞老人也会给你送一件礼物的。"

11. 朵拉上床睡觉以后，亚瑟把一块奶酪放进了快快的笼子里，自言自语地说："万一圣诞老人忘记了呢。"

12. 第二天早上，朵拉跑下楼，想看看圣诞老人给她送来了什么礼物，可是她第一眼看到的就是快快的鼠笼——里面空荡荡的！

"快来人呀！"她哭喊起来，"快快不见了！"

13. 全家人都跑过来，他们检查了沙发底下，翻遍了客厅的每个角落。

朵拉越哭越凶。

14. 亚瑟抬头看看圣诞树。

"瞧！"亚瑟喊，"快快在圣诞树上呢！"

快快单脚站立着，正在啃那块奶酪。

"它真以为自己是芭蕾小明星呀？"亚瑟笑着说。

"是呀，你小看它了吧？"朵拉回应，"我教会它的！"

16. 后来，快快又跑到笼子外面去了三次。

一次，全家人发现它钻进了蛋糕盒子里，正在吃胡萝卜蛋糕。

17. 一次，全家人发现它待在朵拉的娃娃屋里睡大觉。

还有一次，全家人发现它躲进了亚瑟的雪地靴里。

29

18. "我真高兴，明天就开学了，"妈妈说，"我可不想再看见小沙鼠了。"

"我要把快快打扮得漂漂亮亮的明天上学去。"朵拉回应。

19. "我要给它洗个泡泡浴。"

朵拉的"泡泡浴"刚说出口，快快就像闪电一样跳起来！

21. 朵拉和妈妈四处寻找。

亚瑟和爸爸也加入了搜索行动。

他们把楼上楼下都找遍了，把每个盒子、抽屉和橱柜也都找遍了，可是谁都没发现快快。

"我再也没法去上学了！"朵拉哭着说。

"别担心，"亚瑟安慰妹妹，"它自己会出来的。"其实亚瑟一样也很担心。

22. 朵拉该上床睡觉了。

"明天，每个同学都会怪我，因为我把快快弄丢了！"她说完就难过地一头钻进被窝。

忽然，朵拉觉得碰到了什么暖呼呼、毛茸茸的东西。

23. "是快快！"她激动地喊。

真的是快快！它正在朵拉的床上躲猫猫呢！

24. 朵拉带着快快和小鼠笼来到学校。

"它是不是给你添了很多麻烦呀？"摩根老师问。

"小菜一碟！"朵拉回答。

ARTHUR and the NEW KID

不一样的新同学

（美）马克·布朗　绘著

范晓星　译

CHISO 新疆青少年出版社

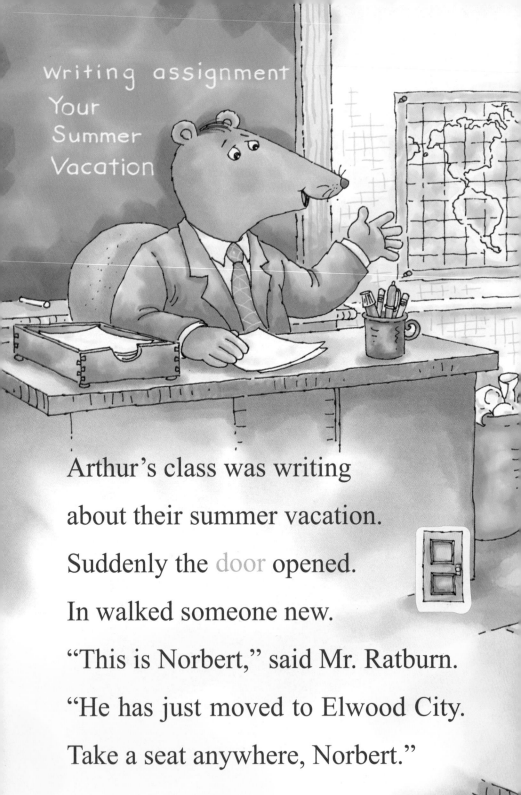

Arthur's class was writing

about their summer vacation.

Suddenly the door opened.

In walked someone new.

"This is Norbert," said Mr. Ratburn.

"He has just moved to Elwood City.

Take a seat anywhere, Norbert."

2

3

Norbert took a seat
in the back near no one.
"He thinks he's too good for us,"
whispered Francine.
"Yeah," said Buster.
"Look at his jacket."

4

Soon it was lunchtime.

Arthur and his friends

sat together.

"Look," said Muffy.

"Here comes Norbert the Nerd."

Norbert walked right past them.
"He's sitting with fourth graders!"
said the Brain.

"He's stuck up," said Francine.

"Maybe he's just shy," said Arthur.

I bet he's rich," said Francine.

"He doesn't bring his lunch.

He buys two slices of pizza,

a milk shake, and lemon cake."

"Yeah," said Buster.

"He's too cool for this school."

9

After lunch Mr. Ratburn said,
"Norbert, why don't you
sit near the others."
Norbert moved up next to Francine.
"Don't worry," she said.
"I take a bath every night."
Everyone laughed.

"Here's a problem," said Mr. Ratburn.

"If a rooster laid two eggs in a bird nest, five eggs in the pig pen, and three eggs in the barn, how many eggs did the farmer find?"

The class was quiet.

"Put on your thinking caps,"
said Mr. Ratburn.

But no one said a word.

"No answer, no recess,"
said Mr. Ratburn.

Then Norbert whispered something
to Francine.

Francine raised her hand.

"Yes, Francine," said Mr. Ratburn.

"The farmer didn't find any eggs,"
she said. "Roosters don't lay eggs!"

Mr. Ratburn smiled.

"Thank you, Francine," he said.

"Or should I thank Norbert?"

15

At recess Arthur and his friends
played soccer.
Norbert watched Buster kick
the ball off the field.
Norbert jumped up.
He bounced the ball
off his head and back to Buster.
"Wow!" said Francine.
"He's really good."

"Want to play?"

Arthur asked Norbert.

"Sure," he answered.

And he kicked in two goals

before recess ended.

19

Francine ran up to Norbert.

"Thanks for getting us recess.

You're really smart!" she said.

Norbert blushed.

"Oh, that rooster question

is in a riddle book I have,"

he said.

After school Arthur and Buster

asked Norbert to go

to Arthur's house.

"Okay," said Norbert,

and he pulled off his tie.

"I had to wear this tie

and jacket at my last school.

My mother made me wear it today.

But I won't wear it again!"

he said.

"Way to go, Norbert!"

said Arthur and Buster.

"Call me Bert," said Norbert.

"High five!" said Arthur.

And they did.

译文

2. 亚瑟和同学们正在写关于暑期生活的作文。

忽然，门开了，一位新同学走进来。

"这是诺伯特同学，"舒老师介绍说，"他刚刚搬到咱们埃尔伍德镇。找个座位坐下吧，诺伯特。"

4. 诺伯特在教室后面的一张空桌前坐下，旁边一位同学都没有。

"他是不是觉得自己很了不起呀？"芳馨小声嘀咕。

"就是，"巴斯特回应，"瞧他那身小西服！"

6. 午餐时间，亚瑟和伙伴们坐在一起。

"看!"玛菲说，"书呆子诺伯特来了!"

7. 诺伯特从他们身边径直走过去。

"他和四年级的同学坐在一起了!"小灵通说。

"他瞧不起咱们!"芳馨说。

"也许他只不过是害羞吧。"亚瑟回应。

9. "我敢说，他们家一定很有钱。"芳馨说，"他都不带午餐，买了两块披萨、一杯奶昔，还有一块柠檬蛋糕。"

"就是，"巴斯特说，"他可不像咱们学校的学生。"

10. 下午上课，舒老师问新同学：

"诺伯特，你为什么不和同学们坐在一起呢？"

诺伯特换到芳馨身边。

"别担心，"芳馨说，"我每天晚上都洗澡的。"

同学们哈哈大笑。

12. "我这儿有一道题，"舒老师说，"有一只公鸡在鸟巢里生了两个蛋，在猪圈里生了 5 个蛋，在谷仓里生了 3 个蛋，农民伯伯一共可以捡到几个蛋？"

13. 全班鸦雀无声。

"好好动脑筋想想哦！"舒老师说。

还是没人回答。

"没人回答，就别想课间休息了！"舒老师又说。

这时，诺伯特悄悄对芳馨嘀咕了一句什么。

14. 芳馨举起手来。

"好，芳馨，你来回答。"舒老师说。

"农民伯伯一个鸡蛋也捡不到，"芳馨回答，"因为公鸡不会生蛋！"

舒老师笑了，说：

"谢谢你，芳馨，还是应该谢谢诺伯特呢？"

17. 课间休息的时候，亚瑟和伙伴们玩起了踢足球。

诺伯特看到巴斯特不小心把球踢出了操场，猛地跳起来用头对准球一顶，回传给了巴斯特。

"哇！"芳馨说，"他踢得好棒啊！"

18. "想一起玩儿吗？"亚瑟问诺伯特。

"当然。"诺伯特回答。

他在课间休息结束之前，踢进了两个球！

21. 芳馨跑到诺伯特身边，说："谢谢你，不然我们就没有课间休息了。你真聪明！"

诺伯特的脸"刷"地红了。

"哦，那个公鸡的问题呀，我在一本谜语书里读过的。"他回答。

23. 放学了，亚瑟和巴斯特邀请诺伯特一起去亚瑟家玩。

"好啊，"诺伯特高兴地回答，随手把领带扯了下来，"我以前上的那个学校要我们每天穿西装、打领带，所以我妈妈今天也非要我这样穿。不过，以后我再也不这样穿了！"

24. "太棒了，诺伯特！"亚瑟和巴斯特齐声欢呼。

"就叫我阿诺吧！"诺伯特说。

"好，记住了！"亚瑟回答。

"阿诺！"

31

ARTHUR, CLEAN YOUR ROOM!

玩具大搬家

（美）马克·布朗　绘著

范晓星　译

CHISO 新疆青少年出版社

"Mom, I can't find my Bionic Bunny," said Arthur.

"No wonder," Arthur's mother said.

"Look at all this junk!"

"It's not junk," said Arthur.

"It IS junk," she said,

"and I want you to get rid of it—

NOW!"

"But how can I get rid of it?"
asked Arthur.

"Sell it," said D.W.

"You can make big money."

"Have a garage sale," said Mother.

"And have it today."

D.W. helped Arthur carry
boxes of junk outside.
"I've always liked
your Jolly Jingle Maker,"
said D.W. "Can I have it?"
"I'm selling it," said Arthur.

GARAGE
SALE
TODAY

ROCKS

7

1

Buster was the first one there.
"I can't believe you're selling this Bionic Bunny Jet Fighter," said Buster. "I don't have a dollar, but I'll trade you my Bionic Bunny Spy Glasses."

"Your Bionic Bunny Spy Glasses!"
said Arthur. "Okay, great trade!"
Buster ran to his house
to get them.

Then Francine came along with
a wagon filled with comic books.
"My mom is making me get rid
of these," she said sadly.
"Oh, boy, Cool Cat comics!"
said Arthur.
"Wow!" said Francine.
"Is that a real
World Cup Soccer Game?"
"Almost new," said Arthur.
"I'll trade it for your comics."
"All right!" said Francine.

11

News spread, and Arthur's friends

all came with things to trade.

"Binky, that is so cool,"

said Arthur. "What is it?"

"My punching bag," said Binky.

"I want to trade it

for your Sailor Sam Ship."

"Good deal!" said Arthur.

Muffy showed up next.
"You've always liked
my clubhouse flag,"
she said. "Want to trade?"
"Sure," said Arthur.
"Is this cute vest
really yours, Arthur?"
she giggled.
"It's yours now," he said.
"It's never been worn."

The Brain came with a radio.

"It needs a little work," he said.

"I'll trade you my elephant mask," said Sue Ellen.

Prunella traded
her rock star poster.

Fern had a typewriter

that Arthur really liked.

Arthur was happy.

His old stuff was gone.

D.W. ran to the garage.

"You didn't sell your

Jolly Jingle Maker," she said.

"But I got rid of all my other

old stuff," said Arthur.

"I'll count your money,"

said D.W.

"Well," he said,

"I didn't really get money…"

17

"But I got all this great new stuff,"

said Arthur.

"If Mom sees this," said D.W.,

"you are in big trouble."

"You're right," he said,

"but what am I going to do?"

"I have a plan,"

whispered D.W.

Later that day, Arthur's mother
went to check his room.
Arthur followed her up the stairs.
He crossed his fingers
and held his breath.

20

"Good job, Arthur," she said.

"You got rid of all your junk."

Just then they heard a big

CRASH!

They ran to D.W.'s room.

Junk was everywhere.

"Dora Winifred!" shouted Mother.

"What is this mess?"

"It's not a mess," said D.W.

"It's business.

Arthur is paying me rent.

And he owes me a dollar."

23

"I don't have a dollar," said Arthur,

"but how about a trade?"

译文

2."妈妈，我找不到我的无敌超人兔了！"亚瑟说。

"找得到才怪！"妈妈回答，"你看看这些乱七八糟的东西！"

3."不是乱七八糟！"亚瑟嚷嚷。

"就是乱七八糟！"妈妈说，"我命令你把这些东西全部处理掉，立刻，马上！"

4."可我要怎么处理呢？"亚瑟问。

"卖掉呀，"朵拉插嘴说，"你能赚很多钱呢！"

5."在车库外面办一次旧货大甩卖吧，"妈妈回答，"今天就行动！"

6. 朵拉帮亚瑟把整箱整箱的旧玩意儿搬到院子里。

"我一直很喜欢你的小丑音乐盒,"朵拉说,"给我行吗?"

"我还要卖呢。"亚瑟回答。

8. 巴斯特是第一个顾客。

"真不可思议,你要卖无敌超人兔的喷气式战斗机!"巴斯特说,"我没有一块钱,但我可以用无敌超人兔的侦探眼镜和你换。"

9. "你的无敌超人兔侦探眼镜!"亚瑟说,"好,就这么说定了哦!"

巴斯特赶忙跑回家去取他的眼镜。

10. 芳馨拉着小车走来,车里装满了漫画书。

"我妈妈让我把这些东西处理掉。"她难过地说。

"哦,天哪,酷猫漫画书!"亚瑟惊呼。

"哇!"芳馨也惊呼,"这是真正的世界杯足球桌上游戏吗?"

"差不多全新的呢,"亚瑟说,"我用这个和你的漫画书换怎么样?"

"好吧!"芳馨点头答应。

12. 消息传开了，亚瑟的朋友们都拿着东西来找他换。

"大胖，这个东西真酷！"亚瑟说，"是什么呀？"

"这是我的拳击袋，"大胖回答，"我想用它换你的山姆水手船。"

"成交！"亚瑟说。

13. 玛菲也来了。

"你不是一直喜欢我的女孩俱乐部的旗子吗？"她说，"想不想交换？"

"当然了。"亚瑟回答。

"这件小背心好可爱，真是你的吗，亚瑟？"玛菲说着"咯咯"地笑了起来。

"现在归你了！"亚瑟回应说，"我还从来没穿过呢！"

14. 小灵通带来一台收音机，对亚瑟说："只要稍微修一下就可以了。"

"我用大象面具和你换。"苏艾伦说。

15. 普拉带来了她的摇滚歌星海报。

芬儿带来了一台打字机，亚瑟可喜欢了。

16. 亚瑟好开心，他的旧东西全都处理掉了。

朵拉跑到车库前说："你的小丑音乐盒怎么没卖掉？"

"反正其他旧东西都卖光了！"亚瑟回答。

17. "我来数数你赚了多少钱。"朵拉说。

"嗯，"亚瑟小声回应，"其实我都没有赚到钱……"

18. "不过我得到了这么多新宝贝！"亚瑟又说。

19. "要是妈妈看到这些东西，"朵拉说，"你就麻烦了！"

"是啊，"亚瑟回应，"那我该怎么办呢？"

"我有个主意。"朵拉凑到亚瑟耳边小声嘀咕。

20. 下午，妈妈去检查亚瑟的房间，亚瑟紧跟在后面走上楼梯。

他把两根手指交叉成"十"字暗自祈祷，大气都不敢出一口！

21. "干得不错，亚瑟！"妈妈说，"你把那些乱七八糟的旧东西都处理掉了。"

就在这时候，忽然传来"哐当"一声巨响，他们赶忙冲进朵拉的房间。

22. 到处都是乱七八糟的东西！

"朵拉！"妈妈大声喊，"怎么这么乱？"

"不是乱，"朵拉回答，"我是在赚钱呢！亚瑟要给我租金，现在他
欠我一块钱！"

24. "我没有一块钱，"亚瑟
说，"给你一个玩具好不好？"